Hello, Family Members,

Learning to read is one of the most important accomplishments of early childhood. **Hello Reader!** books are designed to help children become skilled readers who like to read. Beginning readers learn to read by remembering frequently used words like "the," "is," and "and"; by using phonics skills to decode new words; and by interpreting picture and text clues. These books provide both the stories children enjoy and the structure they need to read fluently and independently. Here are suggestions for helping your child before, during, and after reading:

- Look at the cover ⌐ ⌐dict
  what the story is ⌐
- Read the story to ⌐
- Encourage your cl
  and phrases.
- Echo read with yo ⌐ ⌐aving
  your child read it

- Have your child th
  recognize right aw ⌐ f we
  know the sounds" ⌐ this
  one?"
- Encourage your cl ⌐ ⌐t new
  words.
- Provide the word for your child when more assistance is needed so that he or she does not struggle and the experience of reading with you is a positive one.
- Encourage your child to have fun by reading with a lot of expression . . . like an actor!

After

- Have your child keep lists of interesting and favorite words.
- Encourage your child to read the books over and over again. Have him or her read to brothers, sisters, grandparents, and even teddy bears. Repeated readings develop confidence in young readers.
- Talk about the stories. Ask and answer questions. Share ideas about the funniest and most interesting characters and events in the stories.

I do hope that you and your child enjoy this book.

—Francie Alexander
Reading Specialist,
Scholastic's Learning Ventures

For Leigh Konak,
with great warmth and affection
— M.B. and G.B.

Special thanks to Laurie Roulston
of the Denver Museum of Natural History
for her expertise

Text copyright © 2000 by Melvin and Gilda Berger.

Photography credits:

Cover: Tim Davis/Stone; pages 1 and 28: Norman Owen Tomalin/Bruce Coleman Inc.; pages 3 and 19: Bryan & Cherry Alexander Photography; pages 4-5: Bryan & Cherry Alexander Photography; insets on page 4, top to bottom: Bryan & Cherry Alexander Photography, E&P Bauer/BAUER/Bruce Coleman Inc., Bryan & Cherry Alexander Photography; pages 6-9: Bryan & Cherry Alexander Photography; inset on page 8: David Rootes/Bryan & Cherry Alexander Photography; pages 10-11: John Hyde/Bryan & Cherry Alexander Photography; page 12: Bryan & Cherry Alexander Photography; page 13: Bill Wood/Bruce Coleman Inc.; pages 14-15: Paul Drummond/Bryan & Cherry Alexander Photography; page 16: Francois Gohier/Photo Researchers, Inc.; pages 17-18: Bryan & Cherry Alexander Photography; page 20: L. Veisman/Bruce Coleman Inc.; pages 21-23: Bryan & Cherry Alexander Photography; pages 24-25: Tim Davis/Stone; page 26: Hans Reinhard/Bryan & Cherry Alexander Photography; page 27: Johnny Johnson/Stone; page 29: Hans Reinhard/Bryan & Cherry Alexander Photography; page 30: M.P. Kahl/Bruce Coleman Inc.; page 31: David Rootes/Bryan & Cherry Alexander Photography; page 32: Mark Jones/Bruce Coleman Inc.; pages 33-37: Bryan & Cherry Alexander Photography; page 39: Clara Calhoun/Bruce Coleman Inc.; page 40: Bryan & Cherry Alexander Photography.

Library of Congress Cataloging-in-Publication Data

Berger, Melvin.
    Brrr! : a book about polar animals / by Melvin and Gilda Berger.
      p. cm. — (Hello reader! Science — Level 3)
      Summary: Simple text and photographs present the physical characteristics, behavior, and habitat of a variety of animals living near the North and South Poles, including hump-back whales, seals, polar bears, and penguins.
    ISBN: 0-439-20165-9 (pbk.)
     1. Zoology—Polar regions—Juvenile literature. [1. Zoology—Polar regions.] I. Berger, Gilda. II. Title. III. Hello science reader! Level 3.

QL104.B47 2000
591.7'0911—dc21
                                         00-020823

12 11 10 9 8 7 6 5 4 3 2 1   00 01 02 03 04 05 06

Printed in the U.S.A.
First printing, December 2000   23

BRRR!

A Book About Polar Animals

by Melvin & Gilda Berger

Hello Reader! Science — Level 3

SCHOLASTIC INC.
New York Toronto London Auckland Sydney
Mexico City New Delhi Hong Kong

CHAPTER 1
Lands of Ice and Snow

When you're at the very top of planet Earth,
you're near the North Pole.
This region is called the Arctic.
It is one of the coldest places on Earth.
Everything is covered with snow and ice.
Brrr!

The North Pole is in the middle of the
Arctic Ocean.
But you'd never know it.
That's because you can't see the water.
It is hidden under a thick layer of solid ice.
Polar bears, arctic foxes, and many other
animals live around the North Pole.

When you're at the very bottom of
planet Earth, you're near the South Pole.
This region is called the Antarctic.
Ice and snow are everywhere.
It's even colder than in the Arctic.
Brrr!

The South Pole is not in the middle
of an ocean.
It's in the middle of a vast body of land.
Still, you can't see rocks or soil.

That's because the ground is buried
under a thick layer of ice.
In some places, the ice is two miles deep!
Penguins live around the South Pole.

Many animals live on the land near
the poles.
But here's a surprise:
Even more animals live *in* the polar seas!

CHAPTER 2
Life in the Seas

The icy waters around the poles are
filled with living creatures.
The most common are tiny animals
called **krill**.
They look like little shrimps drifting
in the water.

Krill are eaten by nearly every animal
that swims in the polar seas.

Whales are the biggest of all
sea animals.
Many of them eat krill.

Humpback whales are giant krill-eaters.

They visit the Arctic and Antarctic every spring.

Like other whales that feast on krill, the humpback does not have teeth. Instead, it has long, thin strips of **baleen** (buh-LEEN).

They hang from its upper jaw like a monster-sized comb.

When feeding, the humpback gulps huge mouthfuls of water. The water is loaded with krill. The whale squeezes the water out through the baleen. The baleen acts like a huge strainer. It traps the krill — which the whale then swallows. Some big whales fill their stomachs with four tons of krill *each day*!

Narwhals are whales that live in the Arctic all year long.
But these whales don't have baleen.
They mainly grab fish with their jaws.

The male narwhal is an odd-looking beast.
It has only one very long tooth, or tusk.
The tusk sticks straight out of its mouth!
No one knows how the narwhal uses its tusk.
But you can be sure it isn't used for chewing!

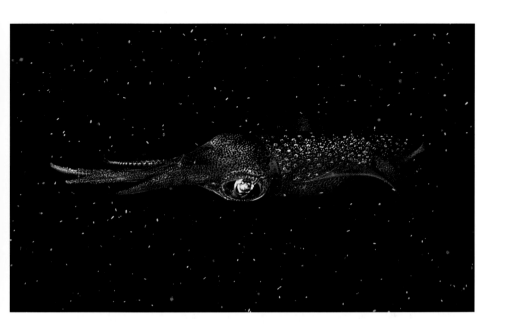

Large groups of **squid** swim in the
polar waters.
Each squid is like an octopus.
But instead of eight arms, the squid has
ten arms coming from its large head.
Squid eat krill, too.
They also use their long arms to catch fish.

Dozens of strange and unusual fish live
in the water around the poles.
Many have big eyes and big mouths.
And most dine on krill.

Some fish have remarkable ways
to keep from freezing in the very
cold water.

The **icefish** and **antarctic cod** have
something in their blood that stops it
from turning to ice.

The substance is like the antifreeze
in a car radiator that keeps the water
from freezing.

Millions of seals live in polar waters.

Ringed seals are found only in the Arctic.

Weddell seals live only in the Antarctic.

Seals feed mostly on krill and fish,

just like whales and squid.

Seals swim under the thick polar ice.

But they breathe air.

So, they need to come up for air every

few minutes.

Can you guess how they do this?

Seals make breathing holes in the ice.
Some chip a hole in the ice with their teeth.
Others scrape away the ice with
their flippers.
A few knock openings in the ice with
their heads.
WHACK!

Every seal has a thick, heavy coat of fur.
The fur keeps the seal warm in the
icy water.
It also keeps the seal's skin dry.
Under its skin, the seal has a very thick
layer of fat, called blubber.
In some seals, the blubber is as thick as
three big telephone books!

Ringed seals are the world's smallest seals.
Many of them swim under the thick
arctic ice.
These seals are the favorite food of the
biggest meat-eaters in the world —
the polar bears!

CHAPTER 3
Polar Bears and
Arctic Foxes

Polar bears live only in the Arctic.
They usually stay on the sea ice.
And they hunt the food they like best —
seals.

A polar bear may wait up to four hours
at a seal's breathing hole.
When a seal comes up for air — *WHAM!*
The bear smacks the seal with its
powerful paw.

Then the bear reaches into the water and hauls out its dinner.
After a meal like this, a polar bear can go without food for about five days.

Polar bears are well fit for life in the Arctic. Their creamy white coats make them hard to see against the ice and snow. This helps them sneak up on the seals.

Heavy fur and a thick layer of fat under their skin keep the bears warm. Also, sharp claws and fur on their paws let polar bears walk on ice without slipping.

During the cold winter months,
polar bears dig dens in the snow.
Here, the female bears give birth
to tiny cubs.
The cubs are much smaller than
human babies.

Female polar bears
care for their cubs
for more than
two years.
They teach the cubs
how to hunt and
find food.

Polar bear cubs grow very fast.
In just a few years, they can be ten feet
long and weigh nearly 1,500 pounds!

Arctic foxes often tag along
after polar bears.
The foxes feed on scraps left over
from the polar bears' meals.
They also hunt **snowshoe hares**
and **arctic hares**.

Arctic foxes change their color
every year.
During the winter, their fur is white.
It blends in with the ice and snow
that cover the Arctic.
In the summer, their coats turn
chocolate-brown.
Then they're hard to spot against
the soil that peeks through the
melting snow.
When winter returns, the color
of their fur changes back to white.

CHAPTER 4
Penguins and Other Birds

Penguins live on the ice of the Antarctic.
They have wings — yet they can't fly!
But the penguins are terrific swimmers
and divers.
They plunge into the icy ocean to catch
their meals of fish, squid, and krill.
Some can stay underwater for up to
six minutes at a time.

After a long dive, penguins shoot up
out of the water.
They look like rockets being launched.
The birds gulp a quick breath of air.
Then they splash back down into
the water.

Sometimes the penguins leap up onto the ice.
Once there, penguins are slow and clumsy walkers.
But they have a way to move quickly.
They drop onto their bellies and push themselves forward with feet and flippers.
ZOOM!
Away they go, sliding across the ice!

The biggest penguins of all are the **emperor penguins**.
They are about as tall and heavy as second graders!
Like other penguins, they spend most of their time diving for food.
When it is time to lay eggs, they jump up and land on the ice.

Each female lays a single egg and heads
back to the water.
Her mate places the egg on his feet and
covers it with a flap of skin.
Then he joins other males in a large circle.
They huddle together to keep warm.

The males keep the eggs on their feet
for a couple of months.
During that time they do not eat.
They lose about half their weight.
Finally, the eggs hatch and the chicks
are born.

By now, the females are back.
They take over the care
of the chicks.
The males march off
to the ocean and
fill their empty stomachs
with food.

In a few weeks, the males return.
Now both parents feed and protect
their chicks.
Six months later, the offspring are
fully grown.
Off they go.
They're big enough to care for themselves.

Many flying birds also live in Antarctica.
Skua (SKOO-uh) are very large and
fierce hunters.
Sometimes they wait near penguin
nesting areas.
They snatch stray penguin chicks
or eggs.
Or, they attack other birds and steal
their food.

Albatrosses are the largest seabirds of all.
They usually breed in large colonies
with thousands of nests together.
The wandering albatross has the biggest
wings of any bird.
Each wing is as long as your bed!
The bird can glide for hours on ocean winds
without flapping its wings.
And it can go for a year or more without
touching down on land.
Quite a record!

The wandering
albatross
mostly eats fish.
But if it is very
hungry, it will
eat dead sea
animals and
floating garbage.

Petrels are cousins of the albatross. One kind, the storm petrel, flies just above the surface of the sea with its legs hanging down. It looks as if it is walking on the water. But you can be sure that it's not!

Arctic terns fly farther than any other bird. In the fall, they head south from the Arctic to the Antarctic.

The birds arrive in time for the antarctic summer.

When summer is over in the Antarctic, the terns head back to the Arctic.

They arrive in time for the arctic summer. Arctic terns have two summers a year — and no winter!

Altogether, they fly 22,000 miles round-trip between the Arctic and Antarctic every year!

Few plant-eaters live in the Antarctic.
That's because the thick ice around the
South Pole never melts.
Almost no plants can grow beneath the
frozen covering.
But many plant-eaters live in the lands
around the Arctic Ocean.

Here the snow and ice melt during the summer months.

Mosses, lichens (LYE-kens), grass, and other low plants grow in the rocky soil, called the tundra.

Large animals, such as **reindeer** and **caribou**, graze on arctic plants.

When snow covers the land, they sniff
the ground for buried moss or lichen.
They use their paws
and snouts to scrape
away the snow.

When winter comes,
some reindeer head
south in giant herds.
Sometimes they walk for hundreds of
miles to reach the forests at the edge
of the Arctic.
The reindeer feed on grass and
tree leaves.
In a few months, the weather starts
to grow warm.
The reindeer trek back north.
And their year starts all over again.

Lemmings are small, chubby plant-eaters. They look like rats covered with long fur. But this is not enough to keep them warm during arctic winters.

When it gets very cold, the lemmings dig burrows in the snow. They feed on plants that poke up into their burrows.

The layer of snow protects the lemmings from the cold and wind. It also hides them from their enemies.

Lemmings breed very quickly. A female can give birth to eight lemmings in just one month!

The number of lemmings in one place grows bigger and bigger. After three or four years, it gets very crowded.

There's not enough food for everyone.

Some lemmings leave to find a less
crowded place to live.
Other lemmings follow.
Soon, millions of lemmings are dashing
away, pushing and shoving as they
rush along.
Many are caught and killed by foxes
or owls.
Some lemmings fall off cliffs.
Others drown while trying to swim across
a river or in the ocean.

In time, there are only a few lemmings left.
Each one has plenty of room.
Each one can find enough plants to eat.

 Once more,
the lemmings
start to breed
and multiply.

From krill to lemmings,

from polar bears to penguins,

all polar animals have their own ways

to survive in the Arctic and the

Antarctic — the coldest places on Earth.

Brrr!